Uncle Aiden

Written and Illustrated
by Laurel Dykstra

BABY BLOCK

VANCOUVER

Inspired by David, Jerry, Matt and Marty

Printed in Canada

Canada Cataloguing in Publication Data:
Dykstra, Laurel
Uncle Aiden / written and illustrated by Laurel Dykstra.
ISBN 0-9738191-0-3
I. Title.
PS8607.Y58U63 2005   jC813'.6   C2005-903550-1

Designed by Bruce Triggs

 BabyBloc Publishing
L102 – 133 Powell St.
Vancouver, BC V6A 1G2
www.babybloc.org

My name is Anna Maria Flannigan Cruz.

I have eleven aunts,

nine uncles

and seventeen cousins.

But I love my Uncle Aiden best.

Uncle Aiden has a red beard,
earrings and big muscles.
He helps sick people.

He is my favorite because

he never gets tired of playing dress-up,

he understands that pretty things
make you feel better

and he doesn't think that having
tea parties is babyish.

Uncle Aiden introduces
me to his boyfriends

and he never misses one of my school concerts.

We do things together

like go to gay pride,

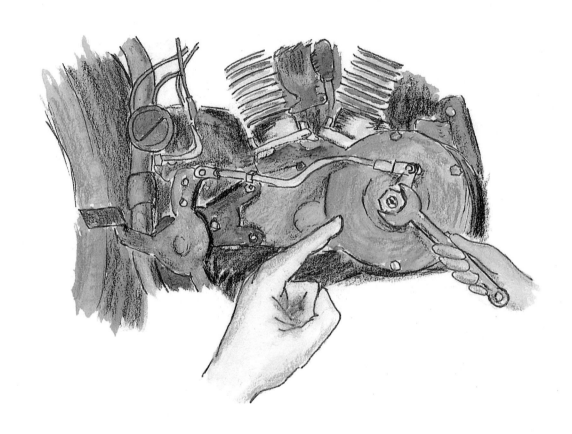

work on his motorcycle,

and play ball.

Uncle Aiden can
throw a ball farther
than anyone in the world,
and he is teaching me how.

I am teaching him Spanish words

like amiga,

gato

and fabulosa.

Uncle Aiden knows things. He says,

"Don't waste your time trying to be
like everyone else,"

"Girls can do anything boys can do,"

and, "Not everyone is going to like you,
what's important is that <u>you</u> like you."

When he makes a mistake he says sorry,

but the best thing about him is
he asks what I think

and he listens to the answer.

I wish everyone had an Uncle Aiden.